ALL-NEW COMICS FROM ALL-STAR CARTOONISTS

MARVEL SUPER STORIES

BOOK 1

EDITED BY JOHN JENNINGS

by Jerry Craft, John Gallagher, Mike Curato, C. G. Esperanza, Gale Galligan, Chris Giarrusso, Nathan Hale, Michael Lee Harris, Ben Hatke, Priya Huq, John Jennings, George O'Connor, Lincoln Peirce, Maria Scrivan, and Jessi Zabarsky

AMULET BOOKS • NEW YORK

TO MIKE PAROBECK, WHO MADE COMICS FUN

ACKNOWLEDGMENTS

It takes a village, if not a universe. Thank you to the following for making this project happen:

Our fifteen amazing contributors—Jerry Craft, John Gallagher, Mike Curato, C. G. Esperanza, Gale Galligan, Chris Giarrusso, Nathan Hale, Michael Lee Harris, Ben Hatke, Priya Huq, John Jennings, George O'Connor, Lincoln Peirce, Maria Scrivan, and Jessi Zabarsky. Thank you for being a part of this anthology and for working these stories into your schedules. You each put the *super* in *Marvel Super Stories*.

At Amulet Books—Charles Kochman and Lydia Nguyen (editorial); Andrew Smith (publisher); Deena Micah Fleming and Brann Garvey (design); Mary O'Mara (managing editor); and Kathy Lovisolo (production).

And last but not least, at Marvel—Sven Larsen, Lauren Bisom, Jeremy West, and Caitlin O'Connell, our weekly (more often than not, *daily*) collaborators.

Cataloging-in-Publication Data has been applied for and may be obtained from the Library of Congress.

ISBN 978-1-4197-6981-8

Book design by Deena Micah Fleming and Brann Garvey

Printed and bound in the United States
10 9 8 7 6 5 4 3 2 1

Amulet Books are available at special discounts when purchased in quantity for premiums and promotions as well as fundraising or educational use. Special editions can also be created to specification. For details, contact specialsales@abramsbooks.com or the address below.

ABRAMS The Art of Books
195 Broadway, New York, NY 10007
abramsbooks.com

CONTENTS

PREFACE

THE PAGE IS A WINDOW

I remember the first Marvel comic book I saw as a little boy. They were comics my mother bought me. Because of my love of folklore and mythology, she thought comics like *The Mighty Thor*; *The Amazing Spider-Man*; *The Incredible Hulk*; and *Daredevil, the Man Without Fear* would keep me engaged with reading.

My mom is a smart woman! And she couldn't have been more correct in her thinking.

I pretty much devoured anything that looked like a comic book after that. It didn't really matter what the story was—I just felt connected and inspired by the artwork and the comics I held with excitement in my hands. My favorite characters have always been the heroes of Marvel Comics. They felt like *friends* to me; like I really knew them.

I learned so much from these super heroes. The writing always had "big words" in them—I'd go look them up in my dictionary so I could follow along. A lot of the characters were doctors, lawyers, and scientists, so they became role models and gave me examples of who I could be when I grew up. I loved that super heroes took care of people. They fought against oppression and evil. They made the world *better.* I really liked that. The mantra "with great power comes great responsibility" really made sense to a young Black kid growing up in rural Mississippi. They were words I lived by.

On top of all this knowledge through action-packed entertainment was the underlying notion of Marvel Comics being a portal to an imaginary New York City—"the world outside your window." I grew up surrounded by thickets of tall grass, dirt roads, and hungry livestock. However, through those comics I started to see other perspectives, other cultures, and New York felt like it was a character in the comics, too.

It would be many years before I got to walk the streets of New York City. I was an adult, but I still felt like a kid seeing the city through the pages of Marvel Comics. I knew that all the neighborhoods depicted in the stories were real, and I caught myself looking for Captain America chasing down a villain, the Mighty Thor flying overhead, or Spider-Man taking a lunch break while perched upside-down on a skyscraper wall.

These days, I try to create comics that make people feel the way I felt as a kid. I want people to see themselves in the characters I write and create. I want people to see what I saw when I opened a Marvel comic book all those years ago.

When you read the stories in this book, I hope you realize that each panel is like a pane in a window. And when you're looking at these awesome super stories, I hope they inspire you.

In the end, each of these characters have a little bit of us in them. That's what makes them so *Marvelous.*

That's what is so *super.*

Each page is a window into ourselves.

—Professor John Jennings

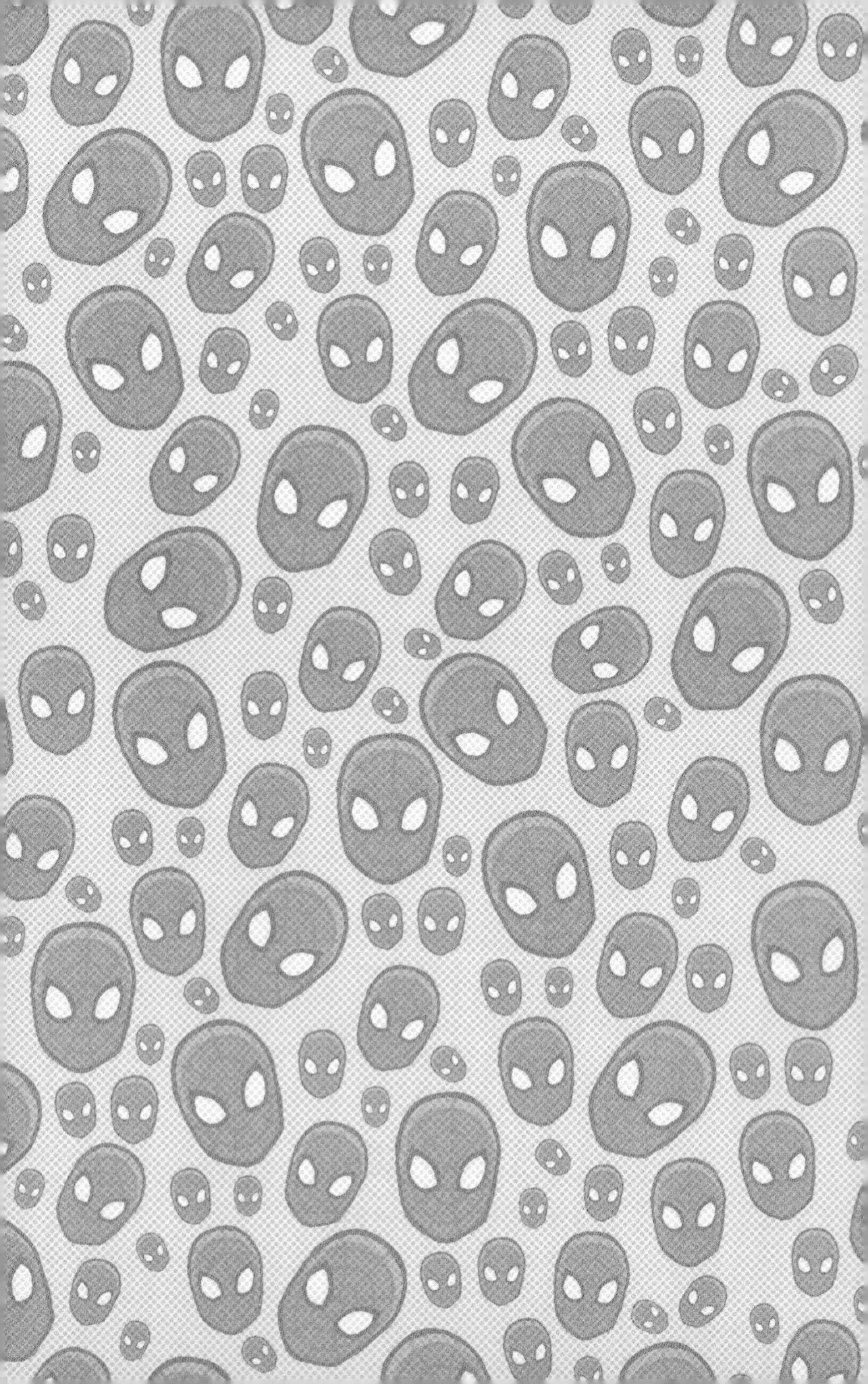

“National Parker”

by

Nathan Hale

Coloring by Lucy Hale

Once a shy science nerd, Peter Parker's life was changed forever when he was bitten by a radioactive spider and given amazing arachnid-like abilities. After the tragic death of his beloved Uncle Ben, Peter realized that with great power comes great responsibility. In addition to looking after his Aunt May, he has since devoted his life to protecting New York City and its citizens as the Amazing Spider-Man!

LAGUARDIA AIRPORT, NEW YORK
PUT MY BAG UP, PLEASE, PETER.
SURE THING, AUNT MAY.
NOW DO HERS.
AND HERS.
AND HIS!
HAPPY TO HELP.
WE'RE GOING TO THE GRAND CANYON.
IT'S ON MY BUCKET LIST!
YOU'RE KIDDING! THAT'S WHERE I'M GOING!
ARE YOU GOING TO RIDE THE BURROS?
YES! I'VE ALWAYS WANTED TO.
BURRO ADVEN
PETER, SAY HELLO TO MY NEW BEST FRIEND.
HI, I'M JUNE. ARE YOU GOING TO RIDE THE BURROS?
I'LL LEAVE THE BURRO RIDING TO THE TWO OF YOU.
I'M FOCUSING ON PHOTOGRAPHY ON THIS TRIP.
OOH, A PHOTOGRAPHER.
PETER HAS PROMISED ME SOME SCENIC SUNSET PICS.
HE USUALLY ONLY TAKES PHOTOS OF CRIME SCENES AND VIGILANTES.
AUNT MAY, I'M A JOURNALIST!
JOURNALISTS CAN'T TAKE PRETTY PICTURES?
I'LL DO MY BEST.
SEVERAL HOURS LATER.
WOW!
SOUTH RIM, BRIGHT ANGEL TRAILHEAD, GRAND CANYON, ARIZONA

THE WEBSITE DIDN'T SAY HOW SMELLY THEY WERE!
I'M FROM QUEENS.
SO I'M USED TO FUNNY SMELLS.
GIDDYAP!
IT'S AN ALL-DAY TRIP, PETER. I'LL MEET YOU BACK HERE.
I'LL BE HERE.
DON'T FORGET, I WANT PRETTY PICTURES.
HUH?
WHOA WHOA WHOA
THWIP
GLAD I PACKED MY SUIT!
WHAT THE—
WHAT'S THIS?! WHOAAA!
CAREFUL!
OH NO! THAT FANNY PACK WASN'T SECURE!
WAAAA
SNAP
AAAAAAAAA
SNAG
HEY! WHAT ARE YOU DOING HERE?
SAVING YOU, SIR!
PLEASE BE MORE CAREFUL!

YIKES!
THESE ROCKS ARE LOOSE!
WATCH OUT BELOW!
HUH?
RUMBLE
CROM
JEEZ! IS EVERYTHING HERE LOOSE?
GOTTA GRAB ON TO SOMETHING!
THWIP
OW!
C'MON, C'MON!
THWIP
RATTLE RATTLE
SNAKE!!!
AAAACHHHHHH
KRUMP
KROMP
KROMP
KROM
MOVE! I CAN SLOW THESE ROCKS, BUT I CAN'T STOP THEM!
WHAT?
YOU SURE PICKED AN UNLUCKY SPOT FOR A SELFIE!
SPIDER—
—MAN?
KROMP
SUPER HEROES VISIT NATIONAL PARKS, TOO!

AAAAAAGH!
SNAKE!
I THREW THAT! SORRY!
SORRY, LIL GUY!
YOINK
YOU HAVE TO BE KIDDING ME!
HELP!
IS TODAY FRIDAY THE THIRTEENTH OR SOMETHING?
HELP!!
SPIDER-MAN!
THANKS! THAT RAPID WAS MUCH BIGGER THAN WE EXPECTED.
EVERYTHING HERE IS BIGGER THAN I EXPECTED!
THANKS, SPIDER-MAN! DO YOU WANT TO CAMP WITH US?
CAN'T TODAY—I NEED TO GET BACK TO THE TOP.
THE TOP? YOU MEAN THE RIM?
THAT'S A FIVE-HOUR HIKE.
NOT FOR SPIDER-MAN!

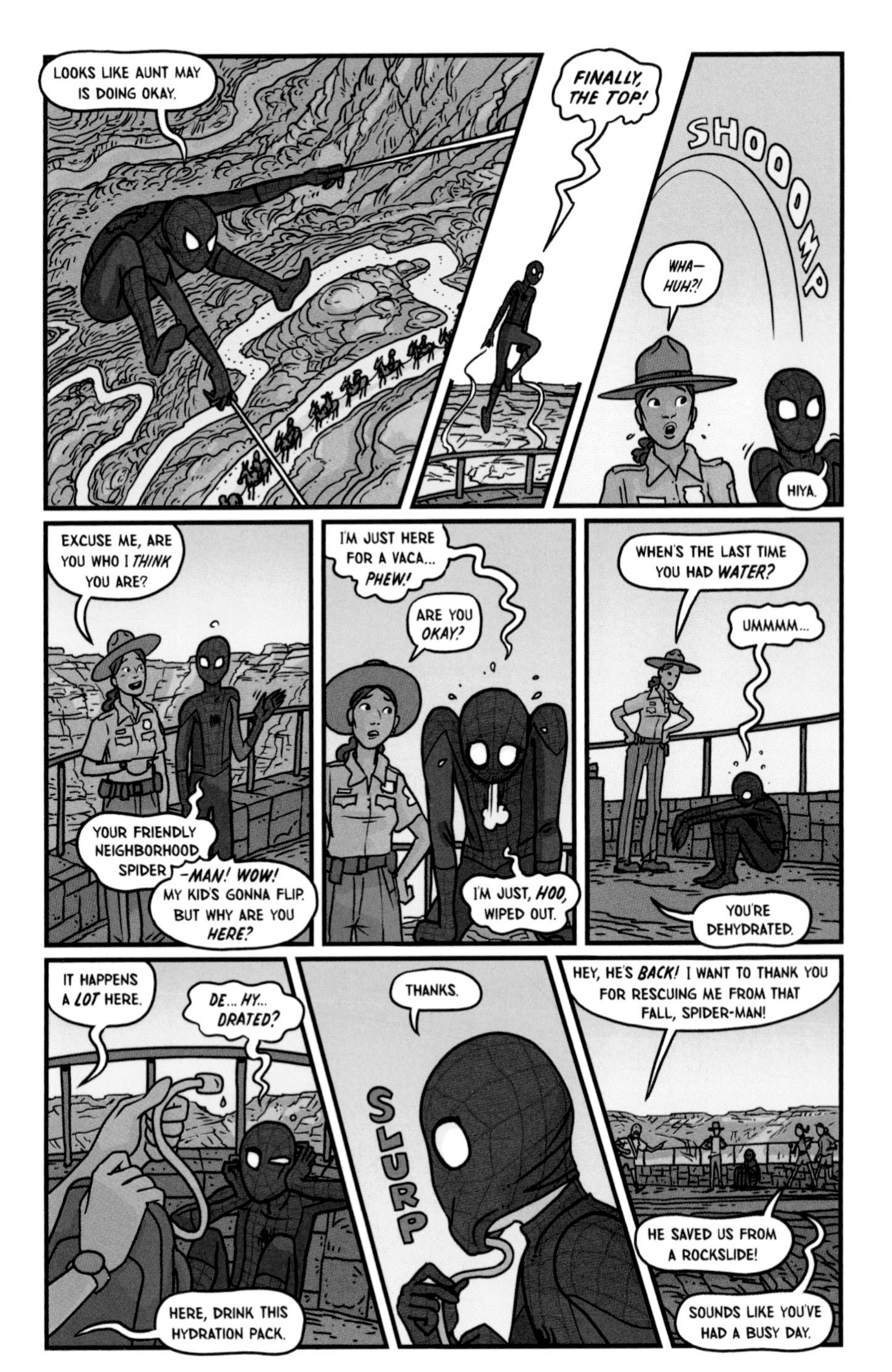
LOOKS LIKE AUNT MAY IS DOING OKAY.
FINALLY, THE TOP!
SHOOOOMP
WHA— HUH?!
HIYA.
EXCUSE ME, ARE YOU WHO I THINK YOU ARE?
YOUR FRIENDLY NEIGHBORHOOD SPIDER
-MAN! WOW! MY KID'S GONNA FLIP. BUT WHY ARE YOU HERE?
I'M JUST HERE FOR A VACA... PHEW!
ARE YOU OKAY?
I'M JUST, HOO, WIPED OUT.
WHEN'S THE LAST TIME YOU HAD WATER?
UMMMM...
YOU'RE DEHYDRATED.
IT HAPPENS A LOT HERE.
DE... HY... DRATED?
HERE, DRINK THIS HYDRATION PACK.
THANKS.
SLURP
HEY, HE'S BACK! I WANT TO THANK YOU FOR RESCUING ME FROM THAT FALL, SPIDER-MAN!
HE SAVED US FROM A ROCKSLIDE!
SOUNDS LIKE YOU'VE HAD A BUSY DAY.

BLACK PANTHER

Monarch of the secluded but technologically advanced African nation of Wakanda, King T'Challa is the Black Panther, a sacred title that must be both inherited and earned by the current Wakandan ruler. Granted superhuman powers by ceremonially consuming a mystical heart-shaped herb, the Panther is responsible for defending his people—and the world—from any threats.

"AS YOU KNOW, SHURI, THIS LIBRARY WAS IN DANGER OF CLOSING BECAUSE OF THEIR FIGHT OVER CENSORING BOOKS. SO WE GAVE THEM THE FUNDING TO TURN IT INTO THE FIRST INTERGALACTIC LIBRARY IN THE UNITED STATES. IT NOW INCLUDES BOOKS FROM NOT ONLY ALL OVER THE WORLD, BUT ALSO FROM ACROSS THE UNIVERSE."

THEY WERE NOT HAPPY, BROTHER?
MOST WERE. BUT THE ONES WHO WERE NOT WERE VERY ANGRY, AND *VERY* LOUD.

WHAT DID THEY SAY?

WE DO **NOT** WANT OUTSIDERS FILLING OUR KIDS' HEADS WITH NONSENSE FROM YOUR COUNTRY.
THE BOOKS ARE NOT ONLY FROM WAKANDA, THEY ARE ALSO FROM THE OTHER 54 COUNTRIES IN AFRICA...
...AS WELL AS EACH COUNTRY ON EARTH AND DOZENS OF CIVILIZATIONS ACROSS THE UNIVERSE.

BUT WE DON'T WANT IT!
SPEAK FOR YOURSELVES! THE WORLD IS CHANGING, AND WE NEED FOR OUR KIDS TO BE A PART OF IT.

WELL IF YOU WON'T LISTEN TO US...

NO
MAYBE YOU'LL LISTEN TO HIM!
WHO WAS IT, T'CHALLA? A POLITICIAN?
NO, SHURI. MUCH WORSE. HE WAS BIG. AND HE WAS VERY, VERY ANGRY.
HE WAS A MEMBER OF SONS OF THE SERPENT.
YOU HEARD THE PEOPLE. THEY DON'T WANT YOU HERE.
I ASSURE YOU, I AM NOT YOUR ENEMY. NONE OF US ARE.
THIS LIBRARY WILL HELP YOUR CITY'S EDUCATION AND ITS ECONOMY.
FOR THE LAST TIME, WE DON'T WANT IT. AND WE DON'T WANT YOU!
THIS MAN IS A HERO WHO HAS RISKED HIS LIFE TO SAVE THIS COUNTRY AND THE WORLD MORE TIMES THAN WE KNOW.
AND TEACHERS AND LIBRARIANS SHOULD NOT HAVE TO RISK OUR LIVES IN ORDER TO TEACH OUR KIDS.
YOU SHOULD BE THE ONES TO LEAVE.
Read.
WELL, IT LOOKS LIKE I'M GONNA HAVE TO ASK YOU WITH MY FISTS. AND BELIEVE ME, IT'S NOT GONNA BE NICE.

DON'T TELL ME YOU HAD A FIGHT. THAT IS NO WAY TO BEHAVE IN A LIBRARY, BROTHER.
NO, IT MOST CERTAINLY IS NOT.
THEN MY ANSWER SHALL ALSO NOT BE NICE!
"I HOPE YOU TREATED HIM JUST LIKE A LIBRARY BOOK, MY KING. FIRST, YOU CHECKED HIM OUT.
WOOSH
"THEN YOU READ HIM...
KRAKK
"...AND FINALLY. YOU RETURNED HIM!
WAKK
"AND I HOPE YOU TOLD THE POLICE TO BOOK HIM ONCE THEY CAME."

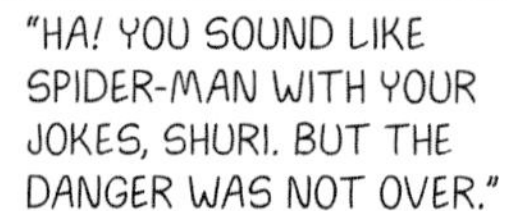

IN ALL THE BATTLES THAT I HAVE EVER HAD, I HAVE SENSED ANGER...AND I HAVE SENSED EVIL.

BUT IT ALWAYS SADDENS ME WHEN I FEEL HATRED FROM THE PEOPLE WHO I AM TRYING TO HELP.

IT MAKES ME FEEL...

...IT'S HARD TO EXPLAIN, BUT I HOPE TO NEVER FEEL IT AGAIN!

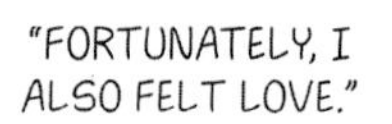

HURRY!
HE SAVED US, MOMMY!
WOOSH
I DON'T NEED YOUR HELP!

ONLY THE STAGE AND BANNERS BURNED. THE LIBRARY IS FINE.
AND THAT IS WHY I INSISTED WE MAKE IT FIREPROOF.
I'M GLAD YOU DID.

"I'M SORRY YOUR EVENT WAS A FAILURE, T'CHALLA."

BLACK PANTHER...
...WAIT!

THANK YOU!

"ACTUALLY, SHURI... IT WAS NOT."

END

"Acorny Situation"

by

Maria Scrivan

Born with unusual squirrel-like characteristics, Doreen Green didn't quite fit in with the super-hero community when she first made her debut as Squirrel Girl. After a series of astonishing victories against the world's greatest villains, she proved herself a force to be reckoned with. The fun-loving heroine balances adventures and school studies while going up against all those who dare to underestimate her and her faithful companion, Tippy-Toe.

TAP! TAP!
TAP!

NOT NOW, TIPPY-TOE! WE HAVE TO GET READY FOR THE SCHOOL DANCE!
CHIKKA CHIT!

THORI CHASED MR. FRECKLE, NUTSO, AND SLIPPY PETE UP A TREE?
CHIKKA!

THAT NUT! BULLIES ARE THE WORST! LET'S GO!

ARF! ARF! ARF!

WE HAVE TO DISTRACT HIM!

THORI, FETCH!

DOGGONNIT! HE'S BRINGING IT BACK!
GRR!

WE NEED A PLAN.

WHERE'S YOUR STASH?
CHIKKA CHIT!

I KNOW YOU'VE BEEN SAVING THEM ALL WINTER. I'LL GET YOU SOME PEANUT BUTTER.
CHIKKA?
YES, A WHOLE JAR.

I'LL DISTRACT HIM. AND WHEN HE'S UNDER THE TREE, WHAMMO!
CHIKKA.

HEY, THORI! WANT A TREAT?

TIPPY TOE, NOW!

FWUMP!

GOTCHA!

NOW SIT.
AND STAY!

LET'S GET YOU BACK HOME!

THOR—COME GET YOUR PUP! THERE ARE LEASH LAWS, YOU KNOW!
UGH, DID LOKI LET HIM OUT AGAIN?! THANKS, SQUIRREL GIRL. I'LL BE RIGHT THERE.

OKAY, YOU'RE SAFE!

NOW LET'S GET TO THE DANCE!

CHIKKA CHIT?
IT'S RIGHT HERE.

NOM
NOM
NOM
PEANUT BUTTER

PEANUT BUTTER

CHIKKA!
CHIT!
PEANUT BUTTER

WELL, THERE GOES MY DATE!
HIC!
URP.
PEANUT BUTTER
END

hawkeye

"Gosh, I Love Arrows"

by

Ben Hatke

hawkeye

Trained at an early age in the art of archery, the young Clint Barton became one of the world's most elite marksmen. Inspired by the selfless deeds of heroes such as Iron Man and Captain America, Barton donned a costume and put his sharpshooting skills to work as the heroic Hawkeye. Young Avenger Kate Bishop also goes by the name Hawkeye. They can get on each other's nerves but make a great team.

WHUMP
I GOT GOOD NEWS AND I GOT BAD NEWS, KATE.

SO...
WHAT'S THE GOOD NEWS?

OUR GUY ON THE INSIDE GOT THE INFORMATION. BUYERS, SELLERS, THE WHOLE DEAL. WE'LL BE ABLE TO TAKE DOWN THE ENTIRE UNDERGROUND PET KIDNAPPING RING.
BAD NEWS?

OUR GUY GOT CAUGHT. HE'S IN THERE.

"WITH THOSE GUYS."
BRO, BRO, BRO.
WE GOT YOU NOW, BRO!

UGH. CLINT. THOSE GUYS ARE THE WORST.

YOU THINK YOU CAN STEAL FROM US, BRO?
WE'LL TEACH YOU NOW!
HA HA!
KICK!

YOU KNOW WHAT I LOVE ABOUT ARCHERY, KATE?
TWO STICKS AND A STRING. THE BOW IS ONE OF HUMANKIND'S OLDEST INVENTIONS.
THERE ARE PICTURES OF BOWS ON CAVE WALLS, KATE.
CAVE WALLS!

HA HA!
WATCH THIS, BRO! RUNNING KICK!
WHIMPER!
THHHP!

KTSH
THHP!
BZZAP!!

BRO, NOOO!

A MOLECULAR DISPLACEMENT ARROW?
VERY "PRE-HISTORIC."

WHAT ABOUT YOU, KATE? WHAT DO YOU LOVE ABOUT ARCHERY?

SIMPLICITY.
ELEGANCE.

THHP!

THHP!

THAK!
HEY!

SNIP!

FLOMP!

NO TRICKS.
JUST TWO STICKS AND A STRING.
WHAT'S THAT, KATE?
TAP TAP.

I SAID—
HANG ON—

THUNK!

FFF!
FFF!

BRO! WHO TURNED OUT THE LIGHTS?!?
KLONK!

I LIKE TRICKS.

TAKE US HOME, KATE.

SNAP!

WOOF.

AW, BRO.

GOSH, I LOVE ARROWS.

END

SNAP!

WOOF.

AW, BRO.

GOSH, I LOVE ARROWS.

END

WHAT IS IT WITH THIS PLACE?
IS IT CURSED?
MUTATED?
THE LAIR OF A SUPER VILLAIN?
THE ONLY VILLAIN HERE IS HUMAN CARELESSNESS.
IF YOU AREN'T CAREFUL AT ALL TIMES, YOU CAN REALLY GET HURT HERE —OR WORSE!
AN AVERAGE OF TWELVE LIVES ARE LOST IN THE GRAND CANYON EVERY YEAR.
MORE WATER?
HERE.
IF YOU EVER WANT TO QUIT THE BIG CITY, WE'D BE GLAD TO TAKE YOU AS A PARK RANGER.
GIVE IT A TRY.
HA HA!
LET'S GET A SELFIE WITH THE SUNSET.
SUNSET!?
OH NO! GOTTA RUN!
ABSOLUTELY GLORIOUS!
WE COULD USE BURROS LIKE THIS IN CENTRAL PARK.
PETER, YOU MISSED OUT!
BUT I JUST CAUGHT THE SUNSET! WAIT UNTIL YOU SEE THESE PICS!
LAS VEGAS AIRPORT, NEVADA
JUNE, WHAT ELSE IS ON YOUR BUCKET LIST?
I WANT TO COME BACK AND RAFT THAT RIVER.
OOH! LET'S GET A BROCHURE!
PETER, AREN'T YOU GLAD WE WENT TO THE GRAND CANYON?
I'M JUST GLAD WE SURVIVED!
END

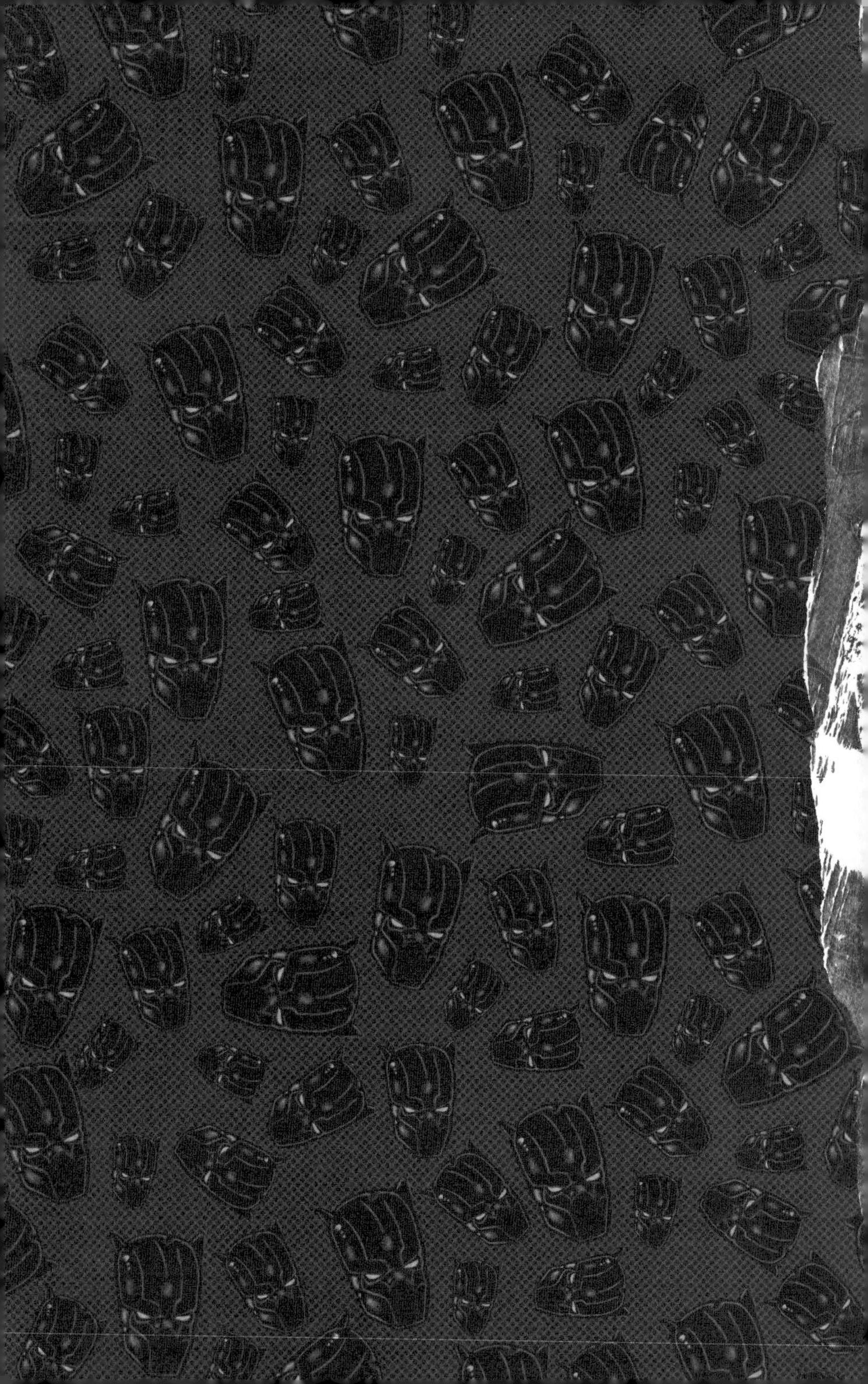

BLACK PANTHER

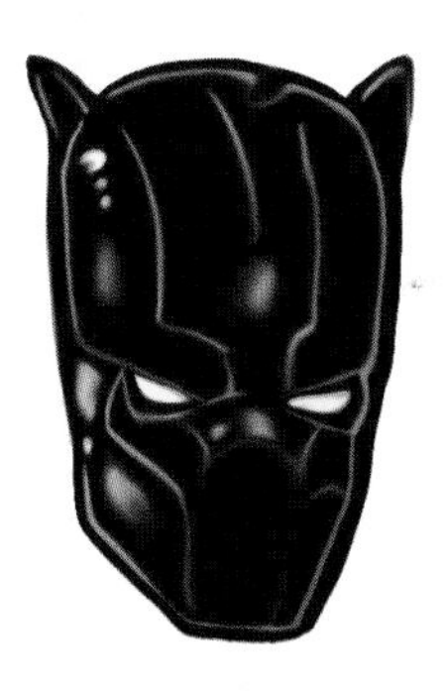

"Banned Together"

by

Jerry Craft

THOR

"Thor's Day"

by
George O'Connor

Legend tells of the son of Odin, heir to the otherworldly throne of Asgard—the Mighty Thor, the mightiest hero of mythology! Once banished to Earth by his father, Odin, in order to learn a lesson in humility, the noble Thor has since vowed to protect the planet, using his enchanted hammer Mjolnir and "mastery of the storm" to vanquish any foes who threaten his adopted home.

Loki was raised in Asgard alongside the Mighty Thor, where he honed his talents of magic and mischief. A trickster and a shape-shifter, Loki is often jealous of his adopted brother, and uses his skills to thwart Thor's heroic plans. Sometimes an ally, and sometimes a foe, Loki's loyalties are always in question, and he is only ever reliably on one side—his own.

Thor. What's there to say about Thor?
WHOSOEVER HOLDS THIS HAMMER, IF THEY BE WORTHY, SHALL POSSESS THE POWER OF THOR
He's the God of Thunder, the favorite son of Odin...
Has a magic hammer, Mjolnir, that can only be lifted by the most worthy.
Whatever that means...
Hold, base varlets! I say thee nay!
Sometimes he talks strangely, too, but honestly he's getting better about that.
Mostly Thor spends his time fighting evil and saving the nine realms from one world-ending threat or another...
Like, just recently. I wasn't actually there myself, but I can tell you how it went down, more or less.

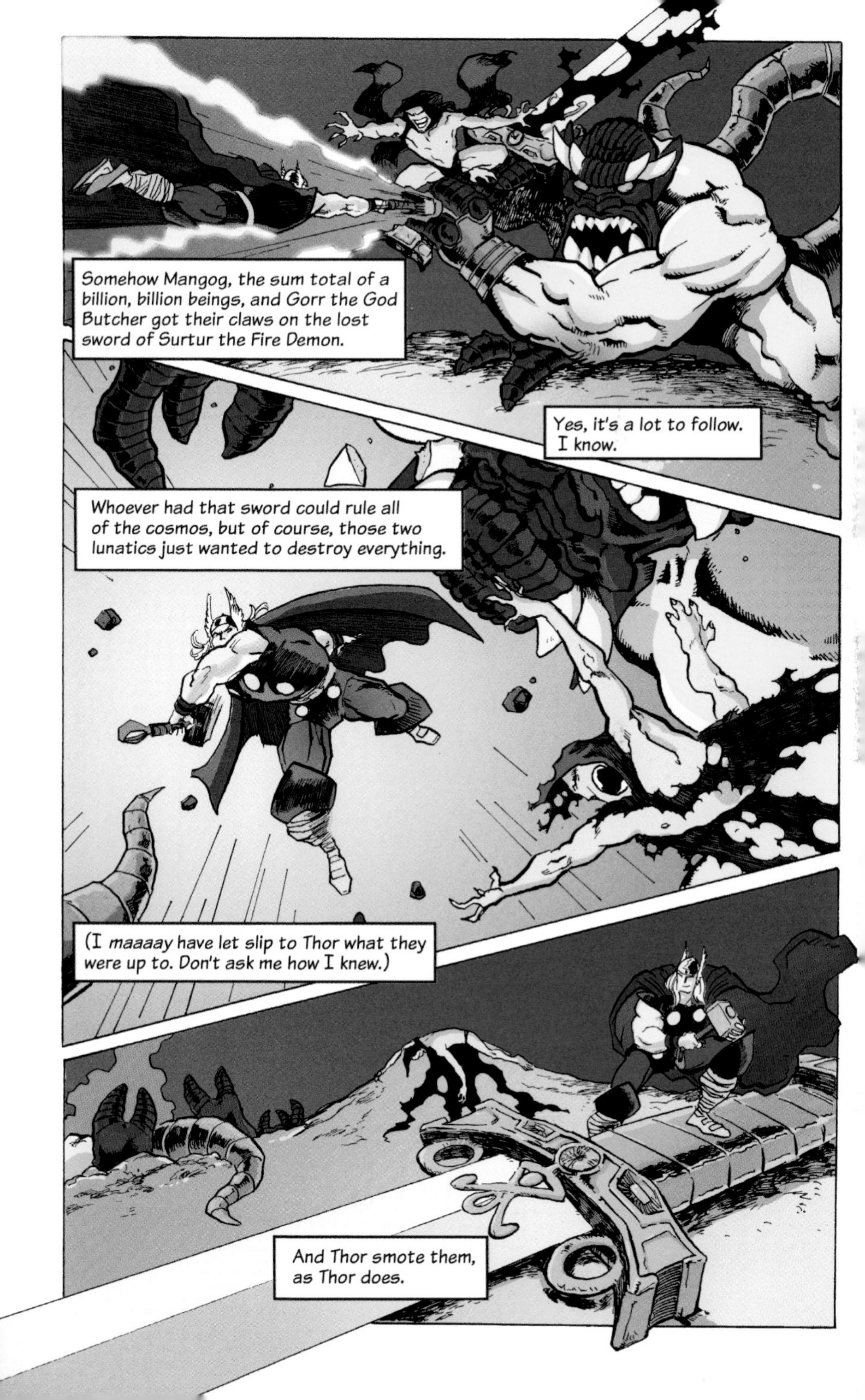
Somehow Mangog, the sum total of a billion, billion beings, and Gorr the God Butcher got their claws on the lost sword of Surtur the Fire Demon.
Yes, it's a lot to follow. I know.
Whoever had that sword could rule all of the cosmos, but of course, those two lunatics just wanted to destroy everything.
(I *maaaay* have let slip to Thor what they were up to. Don't ask me how I knew.)
And Thor smote them, as Thor does.

And all of Asgard, the home of the Gods, was saved, thanks to Thor!
Plucked once more from the jaws of certain doom, the good folk of Asgard wanted to make merry.
THOR'S DAY
And so a celebration was held, the likes of which even ageless Asgard had never seen before, to honor their savior, their hero, their favorite son.
My *brother.*
But where's *my* parade?
All of Asgard is expected to turn out for this celebration honoring the Mighty Thor...
Far be it from Loki, the God of Mischief and Lies, to disappoint.

How shall I dress for *such* an august occasion?
Something old school?
More glam?
Maybe a little femme?
Young at heart?
I may be overthinking this.
Probably best to just come as I am. Casual cool.
After all, I have far bigger decisions to consider.
Such as this: Shall Loki attend Thor's celebration... as a *friend*?
Shall I stand shoulder to shoulder with the virtuous heroes of Asgard, singing the praises of the noble God of Thunder?

I cooould do that.
MORE THOR
Thor is my brother, after all. Even if he does get all the glory.
Stupid Odin.
But the thought of all those do-gooders posing up there before the cheering throngs...

Perhaps there is a place among them for me as well.
But amongst an assemblage of Thor's enemies...
Yes, *that* is a place where I'd have a seat of honor!

For truly, who could count themselves a greater foe of Thor...than *Loki*?
Yes, now that I think upon it, I know how I shall attend. The chance for mischief, for devilry, is too great. I shall—

Loki.
Thor! Ha-hah-Hi!
How long have you been standing there?

Loki, I came to ask if you would join me.
Our people may conduct this spectacle to celebrate my victory over Mangog and Gorr—

—but twas you who alerted me to their dire threat.
I won't ask how you knew, exactly—
That's probably for the best.
But still. There has oft been strife and ill will between us, Loki, but no matter what, you are my beloved brother.
I couldn't have done it without you.

...
That's right. You couldn't have.
Very well, brother. I shall grace your celebration with my... benevolent presence.

My heart sings, but you're not going dressed like that, are you?
What? It's casual cool!
Oh, yes, totally. Verily.
END

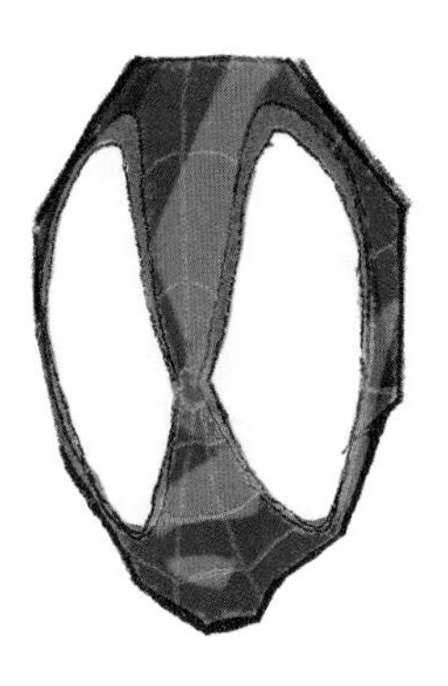

"Spider-Kicks"

by

C. G. Esperanza

Hailing from an alternate world in which Peter Parker sacrificed his life to protect his home of New York City, Miles Morales inherited the mantle (and powers) of Spider-Man when he too was bitten by a genetically altered spider. Though his predecessor's tragic departure left a pair of heroically large shoes to fill, Morales is up to the task, knowing that with great power there must also come great responsibility.

Have you ever worn sneakers so fly that they became part of your *soul*?

I first got these a while ago. I knew great things would happen to me when I wore them.

I was wearing these kicks when I first was bitten by that *spider*!

DONK
That's when I first got my super-powers and became the *new* Spider-Man!
I wore these when I helped my neighbors clean out the lot filled with trash . . .
. . . and turn it into a community garden.
BOM
BA
BOM

I wore these joints when I escaped our family tour in Portugal...
...and then swung from the top of the Moorish castle.
WAK
I wore these in one of my toughest fights against the *Rhino*! I didn't think I could win, but then my kicks came through—literally!

I also wore them that time I spray-painted my first piece on a wall!
PSSST
PSSST
That's why they've got a few drops of paint on 'em.
I think it makes them look even better!

But I guess all things must come to an end. It's been a good ride.

I'll make sure you get a good resting place. Somewhere I can visit you every day and where the city can honor you!

WOOOSH
Ha! Nice try!
GROCERY
WOMP

Try holding them like this and toss 'em backward!

Looks kinda funny, but I'll try it.

SWISH
Every sneaker's got a story, and these two were part of mine.
END

“The Depths of Evil”

by

Lincoln Peirce

Coloring by Tom Racine

King of the underwater realm of Atlantis, Namor the Sub-Mariner has been both friend and foe to the super-hero team the Avengers. Able to breathe on land as well as under water, and gifted with superhuman strength and the ability to fly, Namor is a fierce defender of his people and the ocean ecosystem in which they live. Although he is half-human, he is frequently at odds with humanity over their more destructive tendencies. But he is still an ally when the larger world is at stake.

TELL ME MORE ABOUT THE SURFACE WORLD, NAMOR!

I'VE HEARD RUMORS OF A MAGICAL FOOD CALLED **DONUTS**!
FOCUS, KORI!

IF YOU WANT TO BE AN ATLANTEAN SENTRY, YOU MUST STAY **ALERT** WHILE ON PATROL!
GASP! OVER THERE!
!
!

WHAT'S **THAT**?
LOOKS LIKE AN ***OIL SPILL***!

WILL THE HUMANS **NEVER** TIRE OF POLLUTING OUR OCEAN REALM?
IT DOESN'T **MOVE** LIKE AN OIL SPILL!

CAREFUL! DON'T TOUCH IT!
TOO LATE! IT TOUCHED ME!
GROOANN..
KORI!
WHAT DEVILRY IS THIS? IS HE DEAD?
NOT AT ALL, FISH FACE!
HE'LL SOON BE AS GOOD AS NEW! IN FACT, HE'LL BE BETTER!
CAPTAIN BARRACUDA!
! ! !

"WHAT YOU STUPIDLY CALLED AN OIL SPILL IS ACTUALLY AN ***ARMY OF NANO-BOTS!***

"WHILE WE'VE BEEN CHATTING, THEY'VE REWRITTEN YOUR FRIEND'S *BRAIN PATTERNS*...

KILL NAMOR!
KORI, NO!
I'M SORRY TO HAVE TO DO THIS...
...BUT YOU LEAVE ME NO CHOICE!

BRAVO! NICELY DONE, NAMOR!
OF COURSE, I WAS WELL AWARE THAT A WANNABE SENTRY WOULD NEVER DEFEAT THE MIGHTY SUB-MARINER!...
CLAP CLAP CLAP CLAP

...BUT HE WAS MERELY A TEST CASE! MY TRUSTY NANO-BOTS WILL SOON CLAIM MORE VICTIMS! AND MORE!

AND THEN I'LL HAVE EVERY CREATURE IN ATLANTIS UNDER MY SPELL!

NOT EVERY CREATURE!
WHAT DO YOU MEAN?

FOOOM!
URK!

HOLD STILL, CAP'N!

POW!

WITH THEIR CONNECTION TO CAPTAIN BARRACUDA **SEVERED**, THESE NASTY NANO-BOTS ARE JUST...
...GARBAGE?

EXACTLY. HUMANS MAKE TRASH, AND **WE** CLEAN IT UP... **AS USUAL!**
HEY, Y'KNOW WHAT WOULD MAKE THIS JOB MORE FUN?

DONUTS!
FOCUS, KORI!
END

"Just Captain America"

by

Michael Lee Harris

Lettering by Frank Cvetkovic

Born and raised in Harlem, New York City, Sam Wilson was an intelligent and adventurous child who possessed a great affinity for birds. Later, a chance encounter with the legendary Captain America (Steve Rogers) brought out his inner hero. When the call came for Wilson to join the Avengers, Sam didn't hesitate—he donned a high-tech winged harness and took to the skies as the high-flying Falcon. He has since taken on the mantle of Captain America when his friend is unable to do so.

IT'S THE BOTTOM OF THE SEVENTH...

THE HOME TEAM IS UP AT BAT AND-

HEY! WAIT A MINUTE! YOU CAN'T BE IN HE-

THE SONS OF THE SERPENT HAVE BEEN CENSORED LONG ENOUGH!
SHWEEN
WE WILL NOT BE SILENCED!

WHUMP!
OW!
WHACK
OOF!
WHO'S DOING THAT?
THUMP
KRSSSH!!
CAW!
WHOOSH
AIN' IT SUPPOSED TO BE A BALD EAGLE?

NOT WHAT YOU WERE EXPECTING, *HUNH?*
HOW DARE YOU WEA–
WE REALLY GONNA DO THIS?
MAN, I CAN SEE YOU!

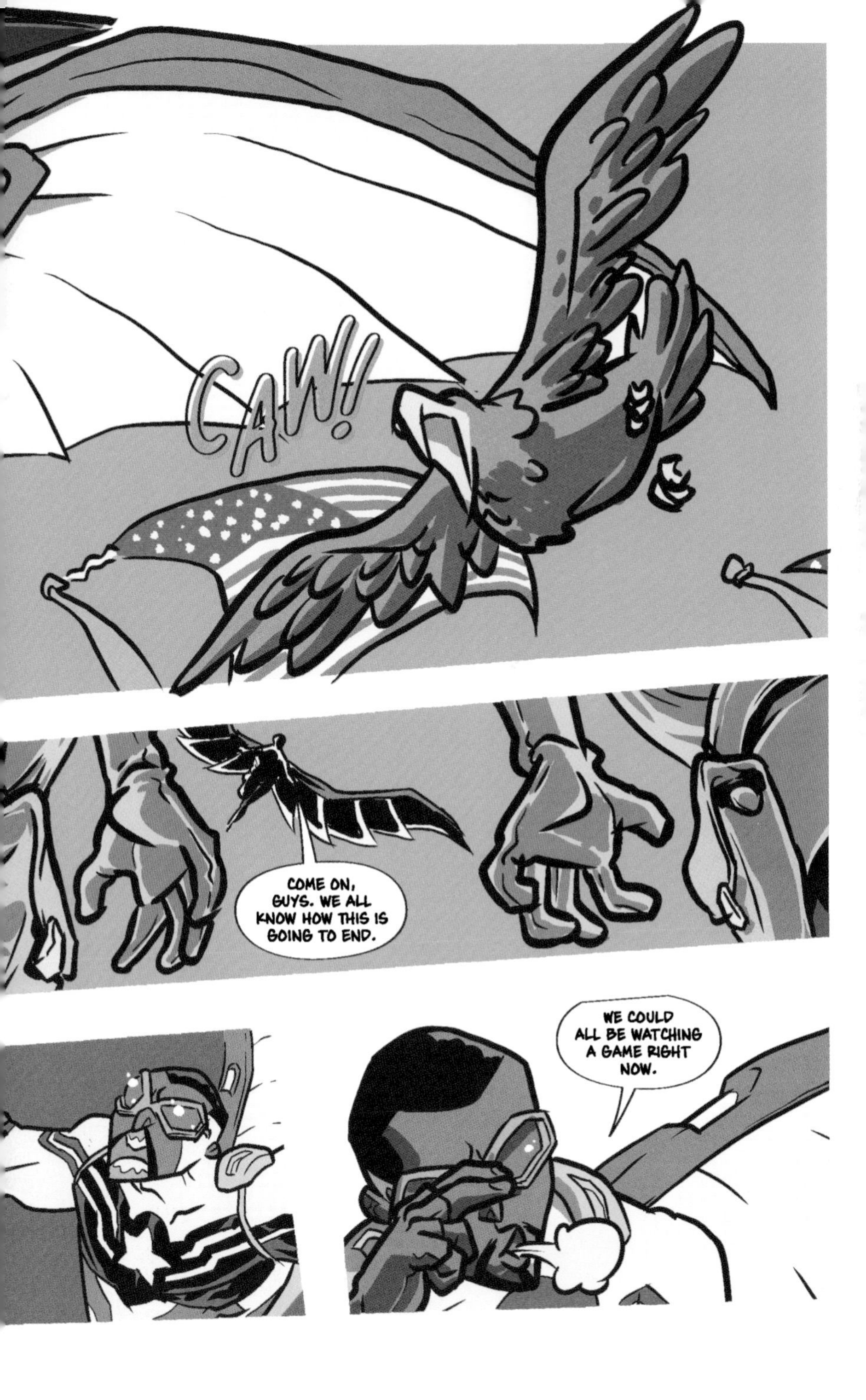
CAW!
COME ON, GUYS. WE ALL KNOW HOW THIS IS GOING TO END.
WE COULD ALL BE WATCHING A GAME RIGHT NOW.

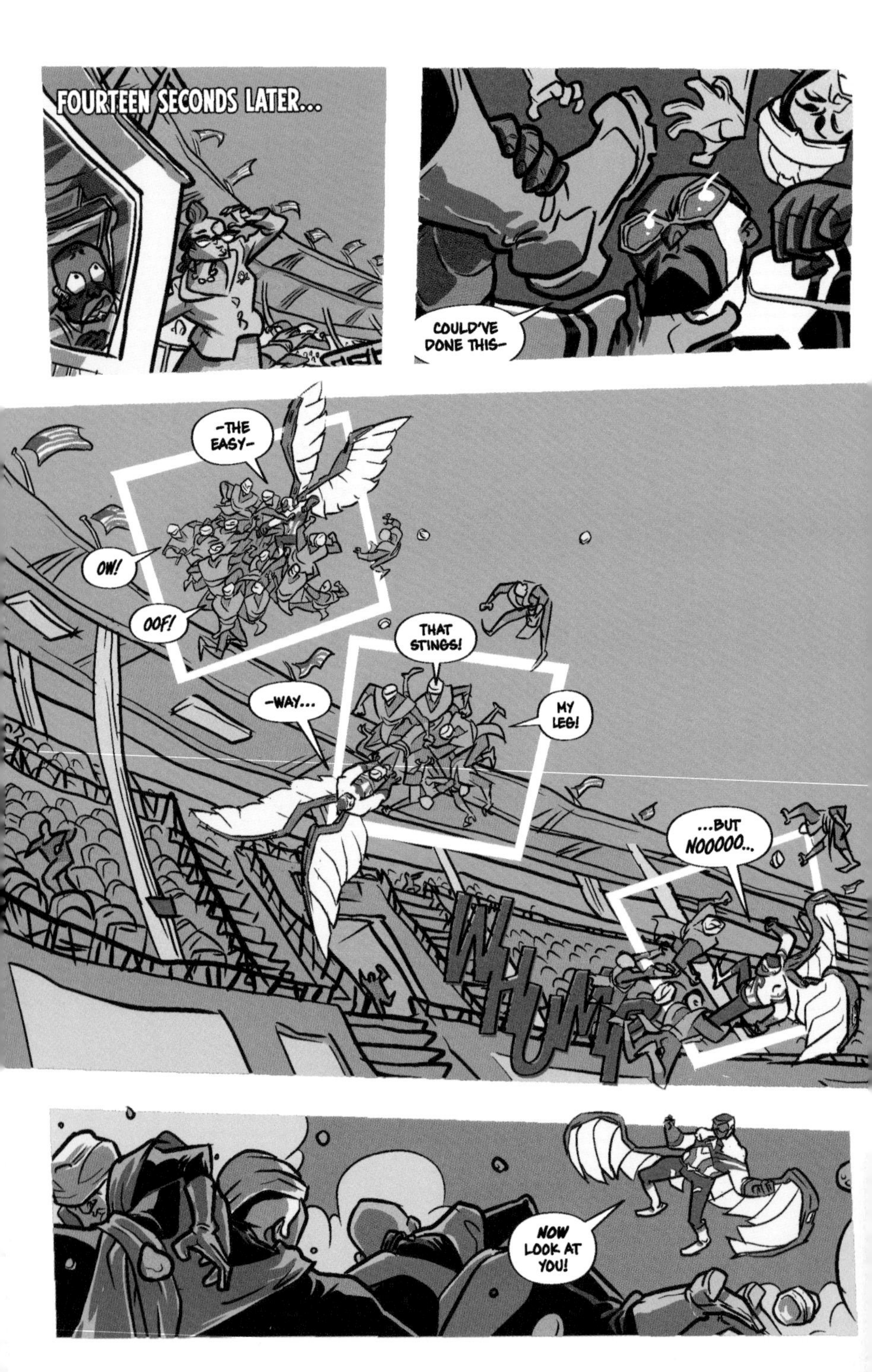
FOURTEEN SECONDS LATER...
COULD'VE DONE THIS-
-THE EASY-
OW!
OOF!
THAT STINGS!
-WAY...
MY LEG!
...BUT NOOOOO...
WHUMP
NOW LOOK AT YOU!

FOUR MINUTES LATER...
POLICE
HE'S RIGHT. THAT WAS A LOT EASIER...
SHUT UP, CLARENCE!

POLICE
HEY, MISTER!

ARE YOU BLACK CAPTAIN AMERICA?

HEH, NO.
IT'S JUST-

CAW!
CAPTAIN AMERICA
END

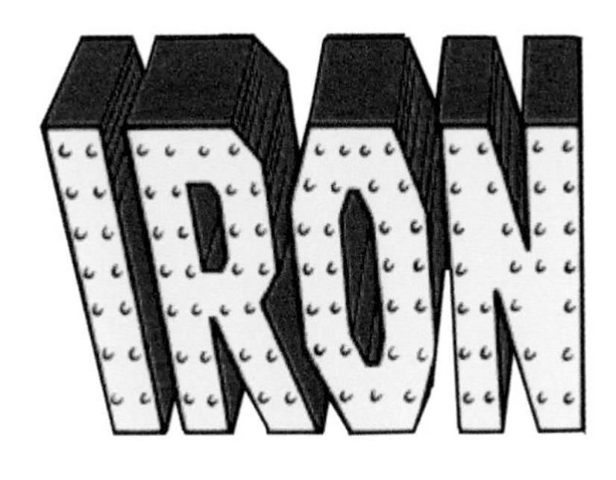

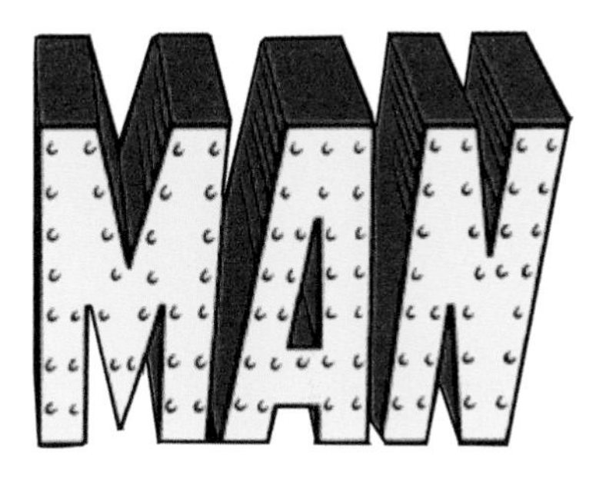

"Blinded by the Light"

by

John Gallagher

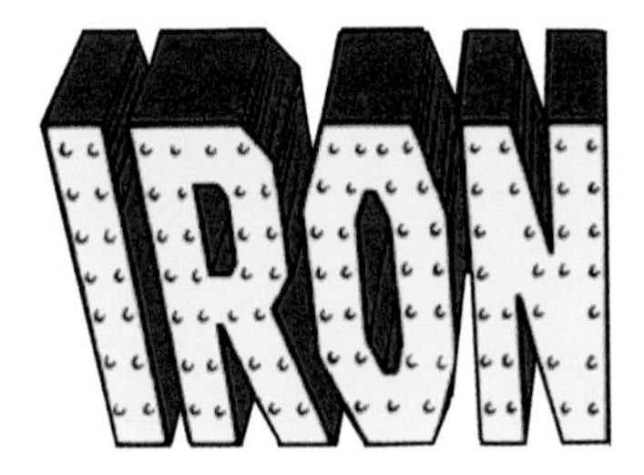

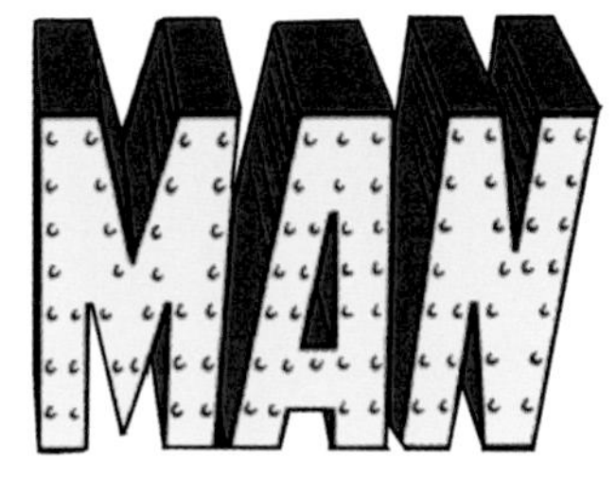

During a violent kidnapping at the hands of terrorists intent on forcing him to build a bomb, billionaire industrialist Tony Stark suffered a near-fatal chest wound. Instead of the weapon his captors had in mind, Stark constructed a sophisticated metal suit that stabilized his injury and allowed him to escape. Upon returning home, he vowed to use his resources and intellect to protect the world as the armored hero Iron Man!

One of my favorite places to visit—Bryce Canyon in Utah.
Unfortunately, there's no time to enjoy the view!
I'm late for the launch of my company's new solar farm!
It looks like this clean energy party's been crashed by my old enemy...
THE LIVING LASER!
That's right, Iron Man—your scientists and workers are my prisoners!

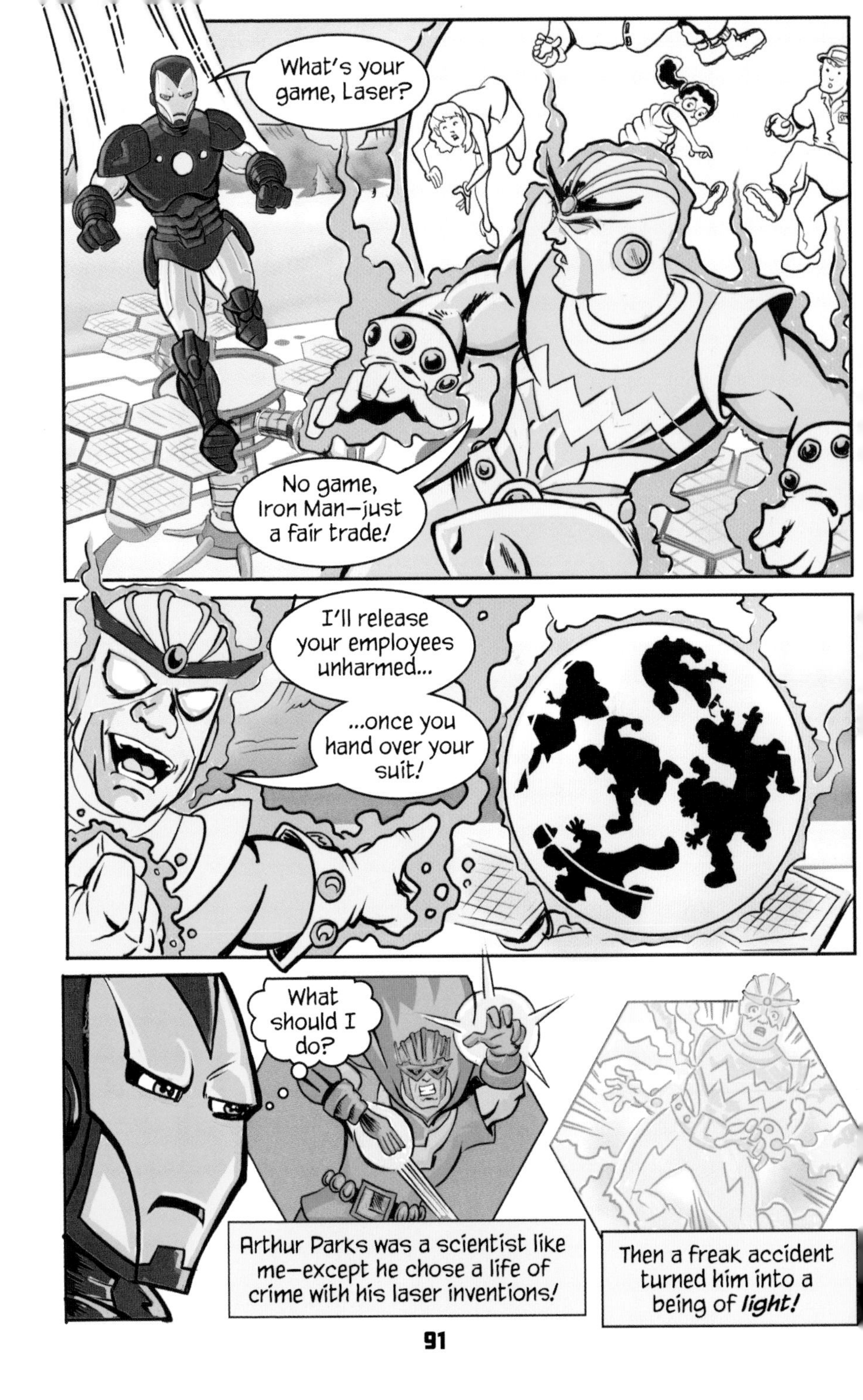
What's your game, Laser?
No game, Iron Man—just a fair trade!
I'll release your employees unharmed...
...once you hand over your suit!
What should I do?
Arthur Parks was a scientist like me—except he chose a life of crime with his laser inventions!
Then a freak accident turned him into a being of ***light!***

Now he's more dangerous than ever!
What do you say, Stark?
Tony! Don't do it!
There has to be another way!
Pepper Potts. My closest friend.
She's in charge of this project for Stark Industies.
And, as usual, she's right.
There's always another way.
Don't listen to her, Stark!
Either you surrender the Iron Man armor or they end up like burnt toast!
Okay, you win.
Suit: Disengage.
But he doesn't need to know my plan.
Yet.

Here you go.
Now disable your ability to control the suit!
Huh?
I'm no dummy. Use your password to disable the remote control.
Well, this is embarrassing.
Okay.
Suit: Disable remote control.
Password: "Pepper-is-Perfect."
STARK INDUSTRIES
Aw, that's so sweet!
Soon.
I've adjusted the suit to multiply my laser powers!
But first, I'll absorb all the power from the solar panels.
Then I'll be unstoppable!
Oh, I wouldn't say that!
Wha—?

You turned the solar panels into a suit?!
That's right, laser brain!
You forgot I designed and invented EVERYTHING my company makes!
If my plan is gonna work, I need to make him angry!
THWACK
You never were smart enough to make your own suit!
SMASH!
I'll destroy your contraption...and YOU, Stark!
Are you sure, Artie?
Perfect—he's mad. And flying right into the center of the solar panels.

And just like I turned the panels into a suit of armor, they can also become...
KRRSHH
CRASH!!!
...a trap!
NOOOOO!
The panels are absorbing my laser power!
Soon.
It's good to get my armor back!
Just in time to help rebuild the solar farm.
You're the boss!
What a waste!
You could have anything you want with that suit!
What else do I need? I get to create fantastic inventions. I've got good friends...
And with their help, I make the world a better place!
Sheesh!
You know, for a guy made of light, Parks isn't too bright!
END

SHANG-CHI 尚氣

"The Café Cat-astrophe!"

by

Gale Galligan

SHANG-CHI 尚氣

Raised by his father, Zheng Zu, as the heir to the villainous Five Weapons Society, Shang-Chi is a master of the Ten Rings and many forms of martial arts. In spite of his upbringing, Shang-Chi's sense of heroism has always been strong. Now he fights alongside the Avengers to protect Earth from all who dare to threaten it.

A RAINY DAY IN NEW YORK CITY'S **CHINATOWN.**
THREE POWERFUL LEADERS OF A **FORMERLY** CRIMINAL ORGANIZATION CONVERGE FROM ACROSS THE WORLD...
...FOR THEIR SUPREME COMMANDER, **SHANG-CHI,** HAS CALLED AN **URGENT MEETING.**

BROTHER, SISTERS...
...WE HAVE BEEN THROUGH A LOT RECENTLY.
WE SURVIVED THE **NEGATIVE ZONE**—
FOUGHT EVERY **SUPER HERO** IN AMERICA—
EVEN FACED DOWN MY GRANDFATHER AND HIS **QILIN RIDERS.**
YET WE'VE STILL ONLY KNOWN ONE ANOTHER FOR, LIKE, TWO MONTHS.
TEA?
YES, PLEASE.
WE MAY BE IN CHARGE OF THE **FIVE WEAPONS SOCIETY...**
...BUT I ALSO WANT US TO SPEND TIME TOGETHER AS A FAMILY.
AND I HAD A GIFT CARD TO THIS CAT CAFÉ.
AHHH.

AND SO...
AW, COME BACK!
rumble rumble
MWARRRR
KOOOOM
Kra
HWAAAAAAH?!
WHAT—
IS—
THAT?!
crash
A GIANT CAT MONSTER, OBVIOUSLY!
THANK YOU FOR THE INSIGHT!
thwa—
KOW

heh
IS THAT ALL YOU'VE GOT?
Mrrrrrrr
hsssss
OH. OH DEAR.
mew mew mew
mew
mew
mew
mew
mew
mew
mew
mew
RINGS OF POWER, I SUMMON Y—
SHANG-CHI, **NO!** DON'T HURT THE CATS!
AAAGH! YOU'RE RIGHT!
AUGHHH!
TAKESHI! ZHILAN! ESME!!
mew
mew
mew
mew
mew
mew
mew
mew

NNNNGH.
YOU—!

WHY DID YOU ATTACK US?
DON'T PRETEND YOU DON'T KNOW.
THE FIVE WEAPONS SOCIETY DESTROYED MY PARENTS.
TOOK ALL WE HAD.
LEFT ME WITHOUT A FAMILY.
SO GO ON...
...FINISH THE JOB.

I'M SO SORRY.
MY PREDECESSOR WAS A MONSTER.

NOTHING CAN BRING YOUR FAMILY BACK. BUT I PROMISE...

...WE WILL DO ALL WE CAN TO MAKE AMENDS.

WHEEEW!

EVEN IF THAT DIDN'T QUITE GO AS PLANNED, I'M GLAD WE MET TODAY.
WE SHOULD DO THIS AGAIN.

A MONTHLY FAMILY DINNER!
MAAAYBE ONE OF US CAN HOST NEXT TIME.
END

"Follow the Leader"

by

Chris Giarrusso

A massive dose of gamma radiation transformed Bruce Banner, the brilliant-but-meek scientist, into the jade giant known as the Incredible Hulk. Often targeted by those who misunderstand him, Hulk prefers to use his immense power to smash the forces of evil, proving to the world that he is the strongest hero there is!

BANNER, YOU'RE SUPPOSED TO BE BUILDING NEW WEAPONS FOR THE MILITARY.
Y'KNOW, TO REPLACE ALL THE WEAPONS YOU DESTROY EVERY TIME YOU BECOME THE HULK!
YET HERE I FIND YOU DRAWING SILLY PICTURES!

THOSE "SILLY PICTURES" ARE DESIGNS FOR THIS, GENERAL ROSS—
—THE MOST IMPORTANT WEAPON I'VE EVER BUILT.

WHY IS THIS ON PAPER? I THOUGHT YOU USED COMPUTERS FOR STUFF LIKE THIS!
I PREFER TO KEEP MY DESIGNS OFF THE COMPUTERS IN CASE SPIES HACK INTO OUR NETWORK.

NONSENSE, BANNER! OUR SECURITY IS UNBREACHABLE! NOBODY COULD POSSIBLY BE SPYING ON US!
UGH! NO WONDER I CAN'T FIND ANY OF BRUCE BANNER'S WORK IN THE MILITARY COMPUTERS!
I MUST SEE HIS NEW WEAPON, BUT HOW?!
MILITARY DATABASE HACKED

WELL, THE WEAPON IS BUILT. WE DON'T NEED THIS ANYMORE.
YES, WE DO! WE STILL NEED THE DESIGNS!
SHRED
SHRED
SHRED

WE HAVEN'T EVEN TESTED THE WEAPON YET!
YOU JUST DESTROYED MONTHS OF WORK!

YOU SHOULD'VE USED THE COMPUTER. IT WOULD'VE BEEN WAY FASTER.

YOU DON'T KNOW...

...THE FIRST THING...
...ABOUARRRGH!
HULK SMASH!

OKAY, MAYBE STAY AWAY FROM THE COMPUTERS FOR NOW!

HULK, NO!
B— BETTY?

PLEASE DON'T HURT MY DAD!
HRMM...

CRASH!
WHAT'D YOU SAY TO HIM THIS TIME?
NOTHING!
HE FLIPPED OUT BECAUSE HE CAN'T UNDERSTAND HOW TO USE A COMPUTER.

THE HULK!
LEAPING RIGHT INTO MY LAP!
THIS IS PERFECT!

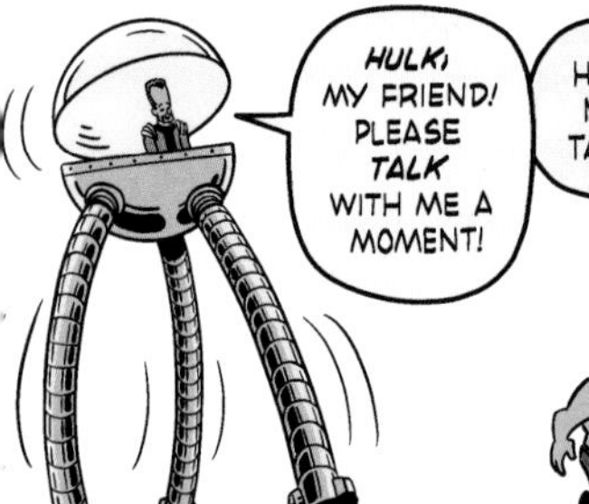
HULK, MY FRIEND! PLEASE TALK WITH ME A MOMENT!
HULK NOT TALK!
HULK NOT HAVE FRIENDS!
HUMANS HATE HULK!
BUT I AM YOUR FRIEND, HULK!
I AM CALLED THE LEADER.

YOU AND I ARE THE SAME, HULK, DON'T YOU SEE?
GAMMA RADIATION TURNED US BOTH GREEN, SO THE HUMANS CALL US MONSTERS AND ATTACK US!
BUT IF WE COMBINE YOUR INCREDIBLE STRENGTH WITH MY INCREDIBLE BRAIN, WE WILL BECOME AN UNSTOPPABLE TEAM!
TOGETHER, WE WILL MAKE THE HUMANS PAY FOR HOW THEY MISTREAT US!
SO SMASH THEM, HULK!
SMASH THE PUNY HUMANS!

HULK NOT WANT TO SMASH ANYONE.

HULK JUST WANT TO BE LEFT ALONE.

THE HUMANS WILL NEVER LEAVE YOU ALONE, HULK!

HEH-HEH... JUST YOU WATCH...
TANK OVERRIDE TARGET:HULK
FIRE

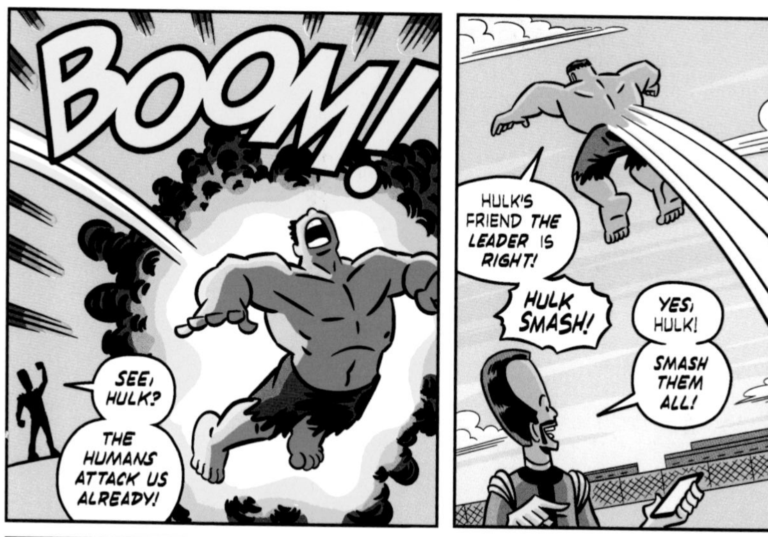
BOOM!
SEE, HULK?
THE HUMANS ATTACK US ALREADY!
HULK'S FRIEND THE LEADER IS RIGHT!
HULK SMASH!
YES, HULK!
SMASH THEM ALL!

KA-SMASH!

CODE GREEN! THE HULK IS ATTACKING US FOR NO REASON!
ACTUALLY, ONE OF OUR TANKS INEXPLICABLY FIRED ON THE HULK FIRST.
YES, ALL TANKS FIRE AT WILL!

BOOM! BOOM!
BOOM!
BOOM! BOOM!

EXCELLENT!
BOOM! SMASH! BOOM!

NOW THAT THE ENTIRE BASE IS PREOCCUPIED WITH THE HULK...

...NOBODY WILL NOTICE ME SLIPPING INTO BANNER'S LAB TO STEAL...

...HA HA!
BANNER'S NEW SECRET WEAPON!

BOOM!
SMASH!

WHA-?
HULK'S FRIEND LEAVING?

WAIT FOR HULK, LEADER!
HULK, YOU MUST STAY AND FIGHT WHILE YOUR LEADER ESCAPES!
NO, LEADER IS HULK'S FRIEND! TAKE HULK WITH YOU!

GET AWAY FROM ME, FOOL!
I'VE GOT WHAT I CAME FOR! I'M DONE WITH YOU!
GLAZAP!

LEADER SHOOT HULK?
HULK THINK MAYBE LEADER LIE TO HULK ABOUT FRIENDSHIP STATUS!
UH-OH...

SNAP!
USELESS WEAPON!
BETTER ESCAPE WHILE I CAN!

NO, LEADER NOT ESCAPE HULK!
HULK...
...WILL
OOOF.

ALL THIS, AND FOR WHAT?
A BROKEN WEAPON THAT DOESN'T EVEN WORK!
IT WORKED EXACTLY AS DESIGNED, GENERAL.
IT TURNED THE HULK BACK INTO ME.

THEN YOU BETTER BE ABLE TO BUILD ANOTHER ONE.
OF COURSE HE CAN!
YOU STILL HAVE THE DESIGNS, RIGHT, BRUCE?
END

WICCAN

“Good Things Come to Those Who Bake”

by

Mike Curato

WICCAN

Son of Scarlet Witch, Billy Kaplan discovered his magical powers when he stood up for himself against bullies at school. He then joined the Young Avengers, a group of heroes taking inspiration from the original super-hero team the Avengers. Wiccan now fights against threats both mystical and galactic alongside his friends and his husband, the shape-shifting hero Hulkling.

MY NAME IS BILLY KAPLAN. BUT THE WORLD KNOWS ME AS WICCAN.
I'M A MAGIC-WIELDING AVENGER BY DAY AND... WELL, STILL THE SAME THING AT NIGHT.
MY MOM IS SORT OF A BIG DEAL SUPER HERO.
MY HUSBAND, TEDDY (AKA HULKLING), IS THE EMPEROR OF AN INTERGALACTIC EMPIRE.
AND I'M SUPPOSED TO ONE DAY BECOME SOME ALL-POWERFUL BEING CALLED THE DEMIURGE.

IT'S KIND OF A LOT OF PRESSURE.

I'VE BATTLED SUPER VILLAINS, ALIENS, AND DEMONS...

...BUT TONIGHT MY GREATEST ENEMY IS MY LACK OF BAKING SKILLS.

IT'S TEDDY'S BIRTHDAY, AND I WANT TO MAKE HIM A CAKE! BUT NOT JUST ANY CAKE... ONE I MAKE *WITHOUT* MAGIC. NO SHORTCUTS!

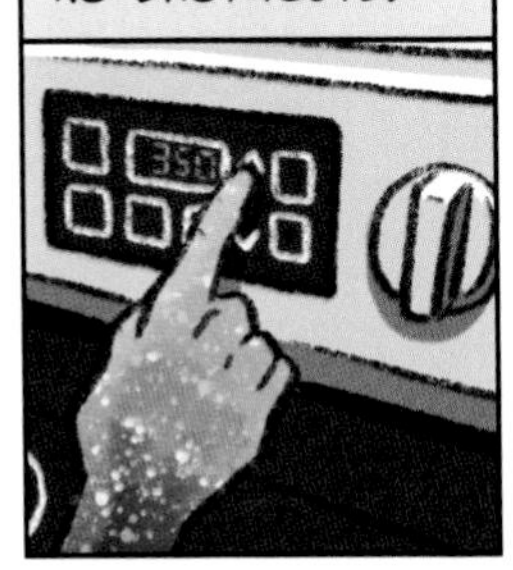

I WANT TO TAKE THE TIME TO SHOW HIM THAT I CARE. IT MAKES ME WONDER, WHAT IF I WERE JUST "**NORMAL**"?

WHAT IF I CAST A SPELL AND GOT RID OF MY POWERS? "*normalnormalnormal*" AND **POOF!** NO MORE **SPELLS**.

NO MORE **FLYING** OR **LIGHTNING BOLTS**. NO **TELEPORTING** THROUGHOUT THE GALAXY SAVING PEOPLE I'VE NEVER MET. JUST REGULAR BILLY KAPLAN, NORMAL GUY AND MEDIOCRE BAKER...

I COULD HAVE NORMAL FRIENDS AND DO NORMAL THINGS, LIKE HAVE A DOG AND BINGE-WATCH AN ENTIRE TV SERIES IN ONE SITTING. I COULD JOIN A VOLLEYBALL TEAM OR LEARN HOW TO KNIT! SOUNDS NICE.

AAAAHH!

THANKS FOR THE SHOES. NOW GIVE US YOUR BAG, *WEIRDO!*

HEY! JUST CUZ YOU HAVE NO FASHION SENSE DOESN'T MEAN YOU CAN STEAL IT FROM OTHERS.
WHAT THE—

GET LOST, *FREAKSHOW!*

YOU'RE *TRIFLING* WITH THE WRONG GUY!

PIE THOSE GUYS
PIE THOSE GUYS
PIE THOSE GUYS
ANYONE WANT *SECONDS?*

I MIGHT NOT BE ABLE TO BAKE A CAKE, BUT I KNOW HOW TO SERVE SOME *"JUST DESSERTS."*

MMM. NOT BAD!

WOW! YOU'RE *WICCAN!* THANK YOU FOR SAVING ME!
ANYTIME, BUDDY.

YOU'RE SO SPECIAL. I WISH I WAS LIKE YOU!
I BET YOU'RE SPECIAL, TOO. AND BELIEVE IT OR NOT...

...I WISH *I* WAS LIKE *YOU.*
BEEP! BEEP! BEEP!
EEK! THE ***CAKE!***

WELL, I DON'T THINK I'M GOING TO OPEN MY OWN BAKERY ANYTIME SOON.

BESIDES, I LOVE WHAT I DO, EVEN IF THAT DOESN'T MAKE ME "NORMAL."

SO I'LL KEEP TRYING TO BE THE BEST SUPER HERO/WORST BAKER I CAN BE.
HAPPY BIRTHDAY!

BILLY! YOU MADE ME A CAKE!

HEH. YEAH. I TRIED TO, ANYWAY. HAPPY BIRTHDAY, TEDDY!

AND I'M ALSO LEARNING...
IT'S SPECIAL, JUST LIKE YOU.
...THAT SOME MAGICAL MOMENTS DON'T REQUIRE ANY SPELLS AT ALL.
END

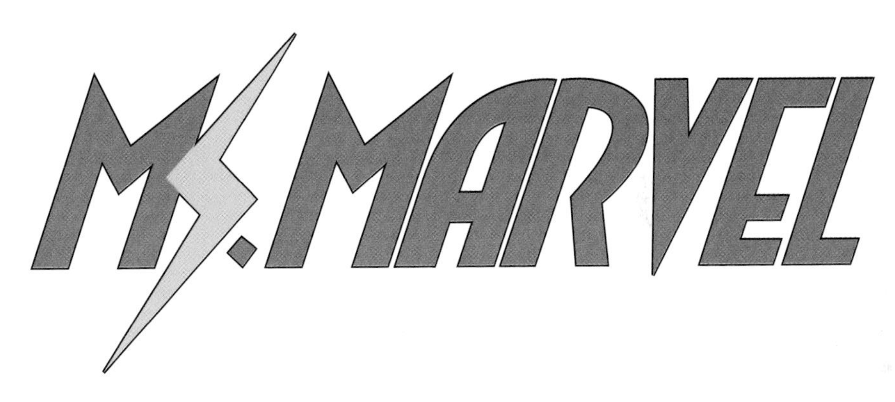

“The B-list Super Hero”

by

Priya Huq

Kamala Khan was once an average teen whose greatest concerns revolved around her over-bearing parents, schoolwork, and her super-hero fan-fiction. When her dormant super-powers manifested, however, Kamala's life turned upside down. Inspired by the heroes she grew up revering, especially her idol, Captain Marvel, Kamala decided to take on a superhuman mantle all her own. She now protects the streets of her hometown, Jersey City, as Ms. Marvel!

I'M A B-LIST SUPER HERO-O-O-O OOO
That's me! I'm Kamala Khan...

Also known as Ms. Marvel!
This is my best friend, Bruno.
And my other best friend, Nakia.
What are you talking about?

There I was, minding my own business...
More like minding other peoples' business...
CHEMISTRY
sociological perspectives

EwTube
WHEN I SAW IT!
IronMansActualSon98:
Ew you like Ms. Marvel?
She's such a b-list super hero
Kamala, you shouldn't take these people so seriously! They're just trolls.
I know, but...

"...What if they're right?"

POW

CRASH

OPEN
mango
3/$5

Come on, Kamala. Snap out of it.

What would **Abu** say?

Your inside problems will ease if you help others.

That's the problem, though. I keep messing up...

Hey, you okay?
Huh? Oh! Y-yeah...

Do you... wanna talk about it?
I... it's so...

I failed my calculus midterm. And I... I feel so stupid and worthless...

I hate myself. I mess everything up!
Don't say that!

I'm sure you're doing your best. Sometimes that feels like it's not enough...

But it is. Doing your best is enough.

Come on, let's go get a snack.

DELI SAN

Maybe I'll always feel like I'm not enough.

But I'm human (well... Inhuman) just like anyone else.

I want everyone to love themselves the way they are.
tap tap
My promise to you?
9:30
Bruno
Nakia
LTE
Hey you feeling any better?
I miss u r u feeling better
YES TY ILY BOTH

I'm gonna love myself the way I am, too!
Love, Ms. Marvel!
END

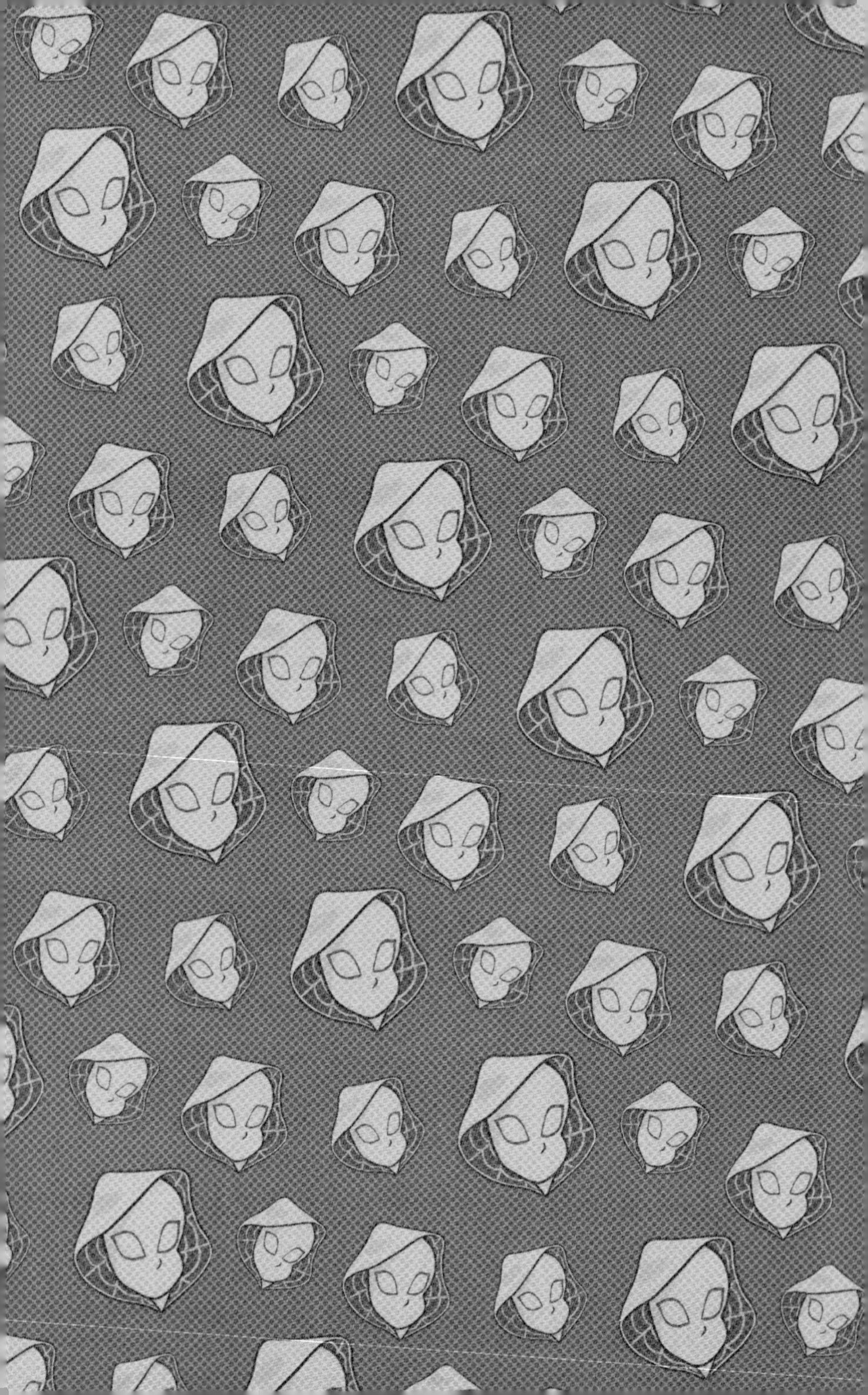

GHOST SPIDER

"Girls Over Ghouls"

by

Jessi Zabarsky

GHOST-SPIDER

In an alternate universe, a twist of fate caused Midtown High student Gwen Stacy to receive the bite of a radioactive spider instead of Peter Parker, granting her amazing arachnid-like abilities. Fighting evildoers as Ghost-Spider, her identity isn't secret, which makes her life even more complicated! Along with her friends Mary Jane Watson, Glory Grant, and Betty Brant, Gwen is an on-again off-again member of the rock band the Mary Janes.

Ugh, I'm late...AGAIN.
I'm so glad I can go to college as a "normal," definitely-not-superpowered teen.
But it was already hard to balance my time.
Now I've got school, new school friends, super heroing, and dad hangouts.
And tonight I'm about to be murdered for missing BAND PRACTICE.

Whew, I'm actually not doing so bad this time!

MJ can't say anything tod—
WOAH!

Oh, C'MON, I was doing so well!

We are destined, Gwen Stacy! Return with me to our home!

Give it UP, creep!

Seriously, Jackal, you need to explore other dating options. Find yourself a nice evil lady.
Give in to fate, Gwen Stacy!
Hey!

Across universes, we are reunited!
Ugh, gross!

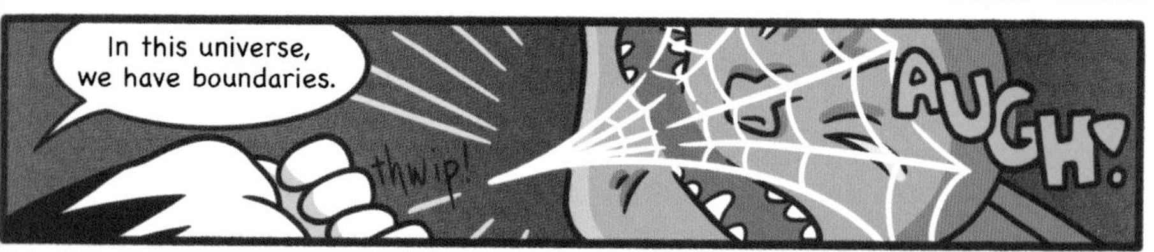
In this universe, we have boundaries.
thwip!
AUGH!

RAUGH!
Whuff
Dude, what good are those goofy ears? I said NO! N! O!
Oh cripes.
CRU—NCH

I shouldn't even be surprised. Gwen has never cared about the band!
That's Mary Jane Watson. In another universe, she's Spider-Man's girlfriend. In this one, she's our passionate band leader.
Aw, MJ, I don't think that's true. Gwen has a lot on her plate right now!
Yeah, we've all had a hard time adjusting to college. And Gwen's got baddie-punching on top of it all.

But the band's IMPORTANT—!

Uffff.

FWWWWEEEEEW

I guess...
she's probably pretty
stressed out...
AAAAAA
Uh...sorry, guys.
Is everyone okay?
THIS jerk?!
HE'S why
you're late?
oogh.
How dare
you!
She's our
DRUMMER,
creep!
UNFORGIVABLE!
Ow!
Oof!
Augh!
Guys...

Listen, thanks. All of you. And I'm really sorry I was late again—

You're off the hook—this ONE time. Because of your stupid STALKER.

But never again!

She's trying, really. Here, fuel up.
Uh, what do we do with him...?
C'MON, LET'S PRACTICE!
Graaaaaa
CHIP
END

"Secret Weapon"

by

John Jennings

Matt Murdock lost his eyesight at a young age when he valiantly pushed a stranger out of the way of a hurtling truck. Though blinded by the vehicle's toxic cargo, Matt soon found that his other senses had been heightened to extraordinary levels. Over the years, he devoted his life to simultaneously studying the law and mastering his unique gifts. Murdock now protects Hell's Kitchen and New York City as both a talented defense attorney and the costumed hero known as Daredevil, the Man Without Fear!

BED STUY, NEW YORK. WILDSEED TECH COOPERATIVE.
I LOVE THIS CITY. IT'S BEAUTIFUL. THE DIVERSITY OF THE PEOPLE MAKES IT SO AMAZING. NEW YORK IS A CITY OF SECOND CHANCES. IT'S WHY I LIVE TO PROTECT IT.
WILDSEED
RIGHT NOW, I AM INSIDE OF THIS TECH CO-OP CALLED WILDSEED. IT'S A REALLY WONDERFUL AFTER-SCHOOL COMMUNITY SPACE THAT TEACHES COMPUTER SCIENCE TO KIDS OF COLOR. TODAY, THOUGH, IT'S MUCH MORE!

BY THE WAY, THEY CALL ME DAREDEVIL, THE MAN WITHOUT FEAR. I'M A SUPER HERO. BUT RIGHT NOW I'M QUIVERING LIKE A LEAF.
SOME REALLY BAD GUYS EXPOSED ME AND THE PEOPLE WHO WORK HERE TO A FEAR CHEMICAL! IT'S TERRIBLE!
THIS GUY IS ONE OF THE SONS OF THE SERPENT. THEY'RE A GANG THAT DOES TERRIBLE THINGS TO PEOPLE WHO THEY THINK ARE DIFFERENT.
THIS SKULL-FACED BADDIE IS CALLED MR. FEAR. IT'S HIS CONCOCTION THAT HAS US FEELING TERRIFIED. WE'VE CROSSED PATHS MANY TIMES BEFORE.
HE'S WORKING FOR THE SONS OF THE SERPENT, AND IS HELPING THEM WITH THEIR EVIL PLAN!
HOW DID WE GET HERE? WELL, IT STARTED EARLIER THIS EVENING...

I HAVE A NOT-SO-HONEST ACQUAINTANCE CALLED TURK WHO, SOMETIMES, PROVIDES INFORMATION THAT HELPS ME FIGHT CRIME. MOST OF THE TIME, I HAVE TO GIVE HIM A BIT OF A PUSH TO HELP ME. BUT TODAY, HE CONTACTED ME AND WAS FAR MORE HELPFUL THAN USUAL.
OKAY, TURK. WHAT DO YOU WANT? I'M A BUSY DEVIL.
MY CONTACTS TOLD ME THAT THE SERPENTS AND MR. FEAR ARE GOING TO STRIKE AT WILDSEED TECH CO-OP THIS EVENING!
THE AFTER-SCHOOL PROGRAM IN BROOKLYN? I KNOW THAT PLACE!
THAT'S THE ONE.
THEY PLAN TO DETONATE A MASSIVE FEAR BOMB AND MAKE PEOPLE HURT ONE ANOTHER.
WHY ARE YOU TELLING ME THIS, TURK? WHAT'S YOUR ANGLE?
MY LITTLE NEPHEW AND HIS FRIENDS HANG OUT THERE. CAN YOU PROTECT THEM?
MY SUPER SPECIAL HEARING TELLS ME HE ISN'T LYING.
I GIVE YOU MY WORD, TURK. I'LL HEAD THERE RIGHT NOW! UNTIL THEN, TRY AND STAY OUT OF TROUBLE!

USING THE CITY'S ROOFTOPS, I MADE IT TO THE CO-OP QUICKLY.
WILDSEED
HOWEVER, WHEN I GOT INTO THE CENTER, THEY USED A BOOBY TRAP —A SONIC DEVICE THAT MOMENTARILY DISRUPTED MY SUPER HEARING! IT WAS EASY TO USE THE FEAR GAS ON ME AFTER THAT!
BUT BACK TO THE PRESENT SITUATION...
THE SONS OF THE SERPENT WILL RULE ONCE THE CITY ERUPTS INTO CHAOS! HAHAHAHA!!
I KNEW YOU'D TRY AND STOP US, DAREDEVIL! THAT'S WHY WE LAID A TRAP!
NOW LOOK AT YOU! YOU'RE SCARED OF YOUR OWN SHADOW!
I HATE TO ADMIT IT, BUT MR. FEAR IS RIGHT! HOW AM I GOING TO STOP THEIR PLAN WHEN I'M PARALYZED BY FEAR?
"MAN WITHOUT FEAR"? HA! YOU'RE SO DISAPPOINTING!

THEN *SOMETHING* HAPPENS! I PICK UP THE SOUNDS OF *STEADY* RHYTHMS WITH MY SUPER HEARING!

IT'S THE *HEARTBEATS* OF THE KIDS! THEY ARE ANXIOUS AND *EXCITED.*
BUT THEY ARE ***NOT AFRAID.*** THE FEAR GAS DOESN'T AFFECT THEM! *AMAZING!*
THEN I HEAR THEIR *VOICES!*

DON'T GIVE UP, *DAREDEVIL!*

YOU'RE OUR HERO! GET UP! ***PLEASE!***

WE *NEED* YOU!

WE NEED YOU!
GET UP!
THEIR WORDS BREAK THROUGH THE EFFECTS OF THE FEAR GAS!

DON'T GIVE UP!
THEIR ***COURAGE*** AND THEIR HEART GIVES ME STRENGTH TO FIGHT. ***I CAN MOVE*** AGAIN!

YOU'RE OUR HERO!
SLOWLY, I RISE TO MY FEET. EVEN THOUGH IT'S TOUGH, ***I DO IT!***

THEN I "EDUCATE" THE **BAD GUYS** ABOUT WHY THEY SHOULDN'T TRY AND **TERRORIZE** PEOPLE.
POW!
TAKE THAT, YOU SNAKES!
ACK!
NOW LET'S **END** THIS! CAN I USE YOUR **JAW** FOR A SECOND? **THANKS!**
UNF!
UGF!

THIS IS IMPOSSIBLE! HOW ARE YOU EVEN DOING THIS?
SMASH
BECAUSE OF WHAT HAPPENED HERE, I RELEARN A VALUABLE LESSON FROM THE KIDS.
IT'S OKAY TO FEEL AFRAID. A HERO DOES THE RIGHT THING IN SPITE OF BEING AFRAID. THESE CHILDREN KNEW THAT AND, IN THE END, THEY WERE MY SECRET WEAPON.
END

ABOUT THE AUTHORS/ILLUSTRATORS

JERRY CRAFT is the #1 *New York Times* bestselling author of *New Kid*, which is the only book ever to win the Newbery Medal (the first graphic novel to receive this honor), the Coretta Scott King Book Award, and the Kirkus Prize. He is also the author of the companion books *Class Act* and *School Trip*. Craft grew up in New York City and is a cofounder of the Schomburg Center's Annual Black Comic Book Festival. He currently lives in Orlando.

MIKE CURATO is the award-winning author and illustrator of the Little Elliot series, *Where Is Bina Bear?*, and the young adult graphic novel *Flamer*. He has illustrated a number of other books for children, including *All the Way to Havana* by Margarita Engle; *Worm Loves Worm* by J. J. Austrian; *The Power of One* by Trudy Ludwig; *What Are You?* by Christian Trimmer; and *What If . . .* and *The Sharey Godmother*, both written by Samantha Berger. He lives in Northampton, Massachusetts.

C. G. ESPERANZA is the author-illustrator of *Red, Yellow, Blue (and a Dash of White, Too!)* and *Boogie, Boogie Y'all*, and the illustrator of *Soul Food Sunday* (which won the Coretta Scott King Book Award). His newest book is *Kicks in the Sky*. He lives in the Bronx.

JOHN GALLAGHER is the creator of the critically acclaimed Max Meow series, the art director of *Ranger Rick* magazine with the National Wildlife Federation, and cofounder of Kids Love Comics, which promotes literacy and the magic of comic books. He also leads workshops teaching kids how to create their own comics. Gallagher lives in Virginia with his wife and three kids.

GALE GALLIGAN is an Asian American cartoonist and comics advocate known for their bestselling graphic novel adaptations of the Baby-Sitters Club and the original graphic novel *Freestyle*. They love making comics that are fun, energetic, and full of heart, and talking about all the amazing things we can learn from graphic novels. Galligan lives in Rockland County, New York.

CHRIS GIARRUSSO began his cartooning career by carving out his own corner of the Marvel Multiverse writing and drawing the *Mini Marvels* comic strips. Giarrusso went on to create the G-Man super hero graphic novel series for young readers as well as *The G-Man Super Journal*. He is currently the illustrator of the Officer Clawsome series, which follows the underwater adventures of a lobster and starfish crimefighting team. Giarrusso lives in North Carolina.

NATHAN HALE is the Eisner-nominated, #1 *New York Times* bestselling author and illustrator of the Nathan Hale's Hazardous Tales series (thirteen books and counting, including *Let's Make History!*). He also wrote and illustrated the graphic novels *One Trick Pony*, *Apocalypse Taco*, and *The Mighty Bite*. He lives in Utah.

MICHAEL LEE HARRIS is a comics artist and illustrator based in Savannah, Georgia. He has worked on titles such as *Choco Leche*, *Gumshoe City*, and *The Most Important Comic Book on Earth*, and contributed to several anthologies. He enjoys writing, drawing comics, storyboarding, illustrating children's books, and talking about himself in the third person.

BEN HATKE is the author of numerous graphic novels and picture books, including the #1 *New York Times* bestselling Zita the Spacegirl trilogy, the Eisner award-winning *Little Robot*, and the underworld journey *Things in the Basement*. Hatke lives, works, and practices archery in Virginia's Shenandoah Valley.

PRIYA HUQ is a Bangladeshi American cartoonist from Austin, Texas, who enjoys working in water-based media. Her debut graphic novel, *Piece by Piece: The Story of Nisrin's Hijab*, was called a "triumph" by the *New York Times*. Her stories deal with complex emotions in both real and fantastic locations. In her free time she likes to drink tea and look at trees. Huq lives in New York City with her spouse and two cats.

JOHN JENNINGS is an award-winning comics editor, author, and illustrator. He is the series curator of Megascope, a graphic novel imprint of Abrams ComicArts, which is dedicated to showcasing works by and about people of color, and the illustrator of *Kindred: A Graphic Novel Adaptation* (a #1 *New York Times* bestseller) and *Parable of the Sower: A Graphic Novel Adaptation* (winner of the Hugo Award). Jennings teaches Media and Cultural Studies at the University of California at Riverside, but his most action-packed role to date is as the father of a real-life super kid, Jaxon Kirby.